KT-449-372

This Walker book belongs to

.....

.....

.....

WALTHAM FOREST LIBRARIES
904 000 00426884

Waltham Forest Libraries	
904 000 00426884	
Askews & Holts	08-May-2015
PIC	£5.99
4648028	5

To Jack,
S.McB.

For Deirdre,
A.J.

First published 2007 by Walker Books Ltd
87 Vauxhall Walk, London SE11 5HJ

This edition published 2015

10 9 8 7 6 5 4 3 2 1

Text © 2007 Sam McBratney
Illustrations © 2007 Anita Jeram

Guess How Much I Love You™ is
a trademark of Walker Books Ltd, London.

The right of Sam McBratney and Anita Jeram to be identified as author and illustrator respectively of this work has been asserted by them in accordance with the Copyright, Designs and Patents Act 1988.

This book has been typeset in Cochin.

Printed and bound in China.

All rights reserved.

British Library Cataloguing in Publication Data: a catalogue record for this book is available from the British Library.

ISBN 978-1-4063-5817-9

www.walker.co.uk

GUESS HOW MUCH I LOVE YOU *in the* SUMMER

Written by
Sam McBratney

Illustrated by
Anita Jeram

WALKER BOOKS
AND SUBSIDIARIES
LONDON • BOSTON • SYDNEY • AUCKLAND

Little Nutbrown Hare
and Big Nutbrown Hare were down
by the river on a summer's day.

On a summer's day there
are colours everywhere.

"Which blue do you like best?"
asked Little Nutbrown Hare.

Big Nutbrown Hare didn't know –
there were so many lovely blues.

"I think ... maybe the sky,"
he said.

Big Nutbrown Hare
looked across the river.
There were grasses and ferns
and tall plants swaying
in the breeze.

"Which green do you
like best?" he asked.

Little Nutbrown Hare began to think,
but he didn't really know.
So many lovely things
were green.

"Maybe the big leaves," he said.

Now it was
Little Nutbrown
Hare's turn to
pick a colour.

He spotted a ladybird, and some poppies.

"What's your favourite
red?" he asked.

Big Nutbrown Hare
thought about red things,
but it was hard to choose
just one.

"I think those
berries," he said.

Big Nutbrown Hare nibbled
a dandelion leaf.

"Which yellow do you
like best?"

There were so many yellows!
Little Nutbrown Hare even
saw some yellows
buzzing about.
How could he
possibly choose?

"Maybe these flowers,"
he said.

Then Little Nutbrown Hare began
to smile and smile.

He looked at Big Nutbrown Hare and said,

"Which brown do you like best?"

And Big Nutbrown Hare smiled too.
There were many many lovely browns,
but one was the best of all...

"Nutbrown!"

Other *Guess How Much I Love You* Books

With more than 28 million copies sold, *Guess How Much I Love You* is one of the world's best-loved picture books.

The endearing simplicity of Sam McBratney's story and Anita Jeram's exquisite watercolours make it a modern classic.

ISBN 978-1-4063-0040-6

Available now

ISBN 978-1-4063-5743-1

ISBN 978-1-4063-5970-1

ISBN 978-1-4063-5428-7

Coming soon to all good booksellers

www.walker.co.uk